W9-AKX-878

FRIENDLY, FROSTY MONSTERS

By P.J. Shaw
Sketches by Tom Brannon
Colorization by Joel Schick

Published by Bendon, Ashland, OH 44805
bendonpub.com
1-888-5-BENDON

Printed in China
82006-TG F 0514

"Yay! Yippee! It's a monstrously snowy day on Sesame Street!"

On with snowsuits and rubber boots. Sometimes you need a big brother—or Big Bird—to help.

Zip and clip!

Clasp and snap!

Wiggle, waggle!

Tussle, tug!

Whee! Whirl!

Slippery-slide on skiddy skates.
Watch out or you'll wobble!

"Oh, dear! Oh, no!" weeps Little Bo-Peep.
"My wooly white sheep ran away in the snow!
Where did they go?"

Run
and
romp!

Baaaa

Slide
and
stomp!

Can you help find all ten?
Plus one shivery black sheep!

Baby Bear slides happily down the hill!
Jack and Jill come tumbling after.

Whish, swish, vroom!

"Ah! I love to count fluffy flakes!
One wonderful flake!
Two terrific flakes!
Three thrilling flakes!
Four fabulous flakes…"

In a wintry wood, Red Riding Hood
enjoys a walk with Bert.
(But beware of that watchful wolf!)

Making friendly, frosty monsters is easy
if you try. Big button eyes—with a snazzy
schnoz or a frosty frown.

Pat! Pack!

Roll it 'round!

Grouches and monsters
like a good, old-fashioned
snowball fight!

Chuck

Huff, puff!

Off with boots, hats,
and monster mittens.
Inside for songs—
and milk for the
three little kittens.

Mmm! Creamy, steamy cocoa!

Then it's time to head home to curl up under a warm, comfy blanket.

Now only moonlight plays on the snow.

Night-night, Elmo!

Snoozzzzzzz...